William S.W. Ruschenberger

# A Biographical Notice of George W. Tryon, Jr.

Conservator of the Conchological Section of the Academy of Natural

Sciences of Philadelphia

William S.W. Ruschenberger

**A Biographical Notice of George W. Tryon, Jr.**
*Conservator of the Conchological Section of the Academy of Natural Sciences of Philadelphia*

ISBN/EAN: 9783337013073

Printed in Europe, USA, Canada, Australia, Japan

Cover: Foto ©Raphael Reischuk / pixelio.de

More available books at **www.hansebooks.com**

Geo. W. Tryon Jr.

A

# BIOGRAPHICAL NOTICE

OF

# GEORGE W. TRYON JR.

CONSERVATOR OF THE CONCHOLOGICAL SECTION OF THE ACADEMY
OF NATURAL SCIENCES OF PHILADELPHIA.

BY

# W. S. W. RUSCHENBERGER, M. D.

[FROM THE PROCEEDINGS OF THE ACADEMY, NOV. 27, 1888.]

## BIOGRAPHICAL NOTICE OF GEORGE W. TRYON, Jr.

### BY W. S. W. RUSCHENBERGER, M. D.

. . . . . " for, go at night or noon,
A friend, whene'er he dies, has died too soon,
And, once we hear the hopeless *He is dead*,
So far as flesh hath knowledge, all is said."

*James Russell Lowell—Agassiz.*

The Academy of Natural Sciences of Philadelphia requested me, February 7th, 1888, to prepare a biographical notice of the late George W. Tryon, Jr. for publication in its *Proceedings*. He died February 5. The suddenness of the event shocked all his personal and many of his merely scientific friends, far and near. One (Mr. C. E. Beddome), who is in every sense qualified to justly appraise his worth, said to me in a note, dated Tasmania, April 4, not very long since received,—" I have respected him as one of the grandest conchologists of the day. I feel that I have lost my most valued correspondent; but what must be the loss of your academy and the conchological world. His great work ' Manual of Conchology,' not yet finished, will be the grandest monument that could be erected to his memory."

Eminence, fairly acquired by a toiler on any path of learning or scientific research, wins admiration, especially from those moving forward on the same quest, whether in his neighborhood or in places widely remote; and after he dies, they become more or less curious about his origin and career. Some are pleased to seek causes of his success in the circumstances of his life, assuming that social environment sways the formation of character, just as physical conditions surrounding certain organisms are supposed to influence their development. Students of this class ask where the eminent man was born and raised and trained, as well as what notable features characterized the locality where he grew to be distinguished among his associates. Those of another sort, who confide almost entirely in the doctrines of heredity, are disposed to ascribe the notable qualities of a contemporary to his parents and their ancestors, thus failing to recognize in him any merit wholly and clearly his own. They seem to forget that uncommon intellectual force, mental capability is not always traceable to heredity or to environment in any considerable extent. All the great heroes of science and literature did not have scientific ancestors or scientific environment. The genius of neither Franklin nor Shakespeare was an inheritance.

George Washington Tryon Jr. the eldest son of Edward K. Tryon and his wife, née Adeline Savitd, was born May 20, 1838, on Green street between Front and Newmarket streets, then in the district of the Northern Liberties. The place of his birth is about twelve or fifteen hundred yards, to the northward and eastward of the State House of Philadelphia,—Independence Hall. The locality was never a fashionable quarter of the city. It abounds in alleys and courts of small tenements, having small windows glazed with eight by ten inch panes, and roofs of cedar shingles, as may be seen to-day. A substantial, industrious people, most of them engaged in mechanical pursuits, inhabited the neighborhood, the alleys and streets of which were the play-grounds of their many children. It is now as it was fifty years ago, only the signs of age in some spots are probably more apparent.

George Washington Tryon, a gunsmith, had trained his son, Edward K. Tryon in the manufacture and trade in fire-arms and sportmen's accoutrements, a business which he had established and conducted successfully during a quarter of a century or more. He retired in 1837, leaving his son in possession of the establishment.

George W. Tryon Jr. at an early age manifested a retiring, cheerful and considerate disposition. His interest in the sports and games of boys was not sufficient to divert him from books. When about seven years old he began to collect specimens of natural history. The taste was encouraged by giving him a room at home in which to display them to members of a society of infant naturalists which he formed. From the start, shells received most of his attention.

The observant and reflective character of the child's mind is notable. He early discovered that a nomenclature was necessary to satisfactorily arrange even a small collection of specimens. He invented one. He named shells according to their shapes or colors, as the round shell, the white shell; one of such irregular form as puzzled him to designate he called the funny shell. The habit of gathering specimens of natural history begun without method in infancy, and more and more systematized as his experience and observation matured, was life-long. His first and predominant love for shells increased with his years and made him an industrious votary of conchology.

He was taught the rudiments of learning at home. After he had passed through one or two private schools for children, it was determined that he should receive academic instruction in the Friends' Central School, because it was regarded to be the best available. It was then in Race between Fourth and Fifth streets, and now is at the S. W. corner of Race and Fifteenth streets.

He became a pupil of the institution in October 1850, and continued till his school days ended, June 1853. During the almost three years here his attention was given only to English studies and drawing. The transfer of the family residence, in 1852, to Pittville, one of the purlieus of Germantown, five or six miles from the business centre of Philadelphia, did not interrupt his regular attendance at school, nor hinder the growth of his museum. The family returned to, and was permanently established in the city, in 1869.

Very soon after leaving the Friends' Central School he employed tutors in the city and studied French, German, and Music until he had acquired knowledge enough, to write and speak the languages sufficiently well for practical purposes, and to understand the principles of musical composition. About this time with some of his young friends he formed a musical society or club. Their performances enlivened the evenings at their country homes.

His interest in books created in him a desire to be an author. His first effort in this direction was a history of the United States finished when he was twelve years old, but not printed. A few years later he announced that literary and scientific work would be his permanent occupation. But, at the earnest request of his parents, he relinquished the project, for a time, and engaged in mercantile work in his father's establishment. At the age of nineteen, 1857, he was given a share in the business, and on the retirement of his father in 1864, he became the principal of the firm, and so continued till 1868, when he retired with a modest income, sufficient in his estimation to justify indulgence in unrestrained pursuit of science and letters.

He found relaxation from business cares in music. Though not a notably skilful player on any instrument, he was acquainted with the science of music.

He wrote a comic opera in three acts, entitled, Amy Cassonet or the Elopement, which was acted at the Amateur Drawing Room, and published; but it was in no sense successful. The copyright is dated, 1875.

He sought to spread a love of music among the people and to elevate their taste. With this in view he joined in the management of the Germania Orchestra for a season. It was a failure. His partner disappeared, and Mr. Tryon had to supply pecuniary deficiencies.

In connection with a musical-publication firm—Lee and Walker,—he edited and published, prior to 1873, librettos of fifty-two standard and popular operas. During 1874 and 1875, he revised and edited the sheet-music publications of Lee and Walker, and in the same years edited The Amateur; a monthly magazine of music and literature. He also arranged a series of operatic songs which were published, in 1875, under the title of Operatic Gems. In 1884, he published "Sacred Songs for Choir and Home Circles, a Collection of Solos, Concerted Pieces, Hymns, etc.," the music of which consisted largely of selections from the scores of the more popular operas.

Mr. Tryon was a warm admirer of the fine arts, and occasionally amused himself with painting.

Music and the fine arts were secondary occupations; they never diverted him from the pursuit of natural history.

He was elected a member of the Academy of Natural Sciences of Philadelphia, June 1859. From that time till the end of his life no one did more to promote the interests of the institution. His services were many and important. The society is largely indebted to Mr. Tryon for the edifice which it now occupies. On his motion, November 14th, 1865, a committee was formed " to devise methods for advancing the prosperity and efficiency of the academy, by the erection of a building" etc. He was appointed chairman of the committee. The measures recommended by it were adopted. The election of a Board of Trustees of the Building Fund followed, Jan. 11, 1867. Mr. Tryon was appointed Secretary and held the office till he died, twenty-one years. He was a member of the building committee. No one labored more assiduously in every way to promote the completion of the enterprise which he had started. He gave $3000 to the building fund; and his generosity enabled the Conchological Section of the Academy to give to it as much more.

Mr. Tryon was elected a Curator of the academy, January, 1869, and resigned July, 1876. Under his direction and personal attention the numerous collections of the museum were safely transferred, in January 1876, from the old, and arranged in the new building. This arduous task was admirably performed

At his instigation the Conchological Section of the Academy of Natural Sciences was founded, December 26, 1866. He was a constituent member, and its Conservator from December, 1875, thirteen years. His skill in conchology is manifest in the admirable arrangement and classification; and his incessant carefulness, in the excellent condition of the collections which were under his official charge. According to the annual report of the Section, December 1887, they consisted of 189,150 specimens, contained in 51,327 trays each with an appropriate label. This enormous collection, and an almost complete conchological library of 954 volumes, besides 455 pamphlets, bound in 26 volumes, all accessible under one roof, render the facilities of study of the subject in the academy unsurpassed.

April 9, 1867, he made a special deposit of more than ten thousand species of shells and more than a hundred jars of specimens, chiefly of naked mollusks, in alcohol, gathered during his life-long devotion to the subject, on condition that none should be loaned. They were appropriately intercalated with the academy's collection. The duplicates were sold, by his direction, and the proceeds of sales covered into the treasury of the Conchological Section. It is notable that he did not stipulate that this very large contribution—the largest private collection in this country—should be kept separate from the rest of the museum and designated by his name, which is a usual condition attached to donations of private natural-history cabinets to public museums. It was his opinion that it is unwise to accept cabinets on such terms, because it must result sooner or later, in encumbering the museum with the care of numberless and useless duplicates, for which space cannot be easily afforded.

The records show that Mr. Tryon contributed valuable specimens to the museum every year during the remainder of his life.

He gave, May 7, 1867, 119 volumes and 56 pamphlets on conchology to the library.

The first number of the American Journal of Conchology, of which Mr. Tryon was the editor and proprietor, was issued, February 1865. Seven volumes were published, the last number in May, 1872. After the institution of the Conchological Section of the Academy it was issued, nominally, by the publication committee of the Section, of which Mr. Tryon was chairman, but he was still the editor. The third and subsequent volumes contain summaries of the proceedings of the Section at its stated meetings.

To the Proceedings of the Academy of Natural Sciences, and to the American Journal of Conchology Mr. Tryon contributed sixty-four papers, between 1861 and 1873, inclusive, a list of which is appended.

In conjunction with Mr. Wm. G. Binney, in 1864, Mr. Tryon edited the complete writings of C. S. Rafinesque on recent and fossil conchology. In 1866, he published A Monograph on the terrestrial mollusca of the United States; in 1870, A Monograph of the Fresh-water univalve mollusca of the United States; in 1873, American Marine Conchology, and A Monograph on the Streptomatidæ (American Melanians) of North America. This work was prepared at the instance of the Smithsonian Institution, and published in its Miscellaneous Collections, in December. It was a result of several years' study. The manuscript was completed in 1865, and laid aside. At the end of seven or eight years, he again took up the subject, which he regarded as " one of the most interesting and difficult branches of American Conchology," and found himself "inclined to question many of the conclusions" which he had reached. In the preface of the work he says:—" A more enlarged acquaintance with fresh-water shells convinces me that a much greater reduction of the number of species than I have attempted must eventually be made; but until the prolific waters of the Southern States have been systematically explored, and a great collection of specimens obtained, which shall represent every portion of those streams and include as many transitional forms as can be procured, a definite monograph of our Melanians cannot be written."

More conclusive evidence of Mr. Tryon's habitual devotion to accuracy in all his work than is contained in the history of the preparation of this monograph is not required.

Mr. Tryon, for the sake of relaxation, left Philadelphia, May 1874, and returned September 19. During an absence of four months, he visited England, Holland, Belgium, Germany, France, Switzerland, Italy.

In a series of letters he wrote good-humored, cheerful sketches of his impressions of people and places at which he halted on his way. They were published in the Amateur; a monthly magazine of Music and Literature.

He visited England and the continent of Europe again in 1877. His route included Liverpool, London, Paris, Marseilles, and thence along the coast of the Mediterranean to Nice, San Remo, Genoa,

Pisa, Rome, Naples, Sorrento; returning through Venice, Florence, Turin, Geneva, Chamouni, Berne, Mayence; the Rhine, Cologne, Brussels, Antwerp and back to London, Liverpool and home, in the autumn.

Now, naturally imbued with the love of truth exclusively for the truth's sake; possessed of the true methods of scientific inquiry, and equipped with the results of his life-long home studies of the mollusca, as well as of his observations in the European museums and cabinets, Mr. Tryon devised the plan of his greatest work—Manual of Conchology—and promptly began its execution.

The plan embraced four series of volumes. The first series of eleven or twelve volumes is devoted to the marine univalves; the second, of six or seven, to the terrestrial mollusca; the third, of four or five, to the marine bivalves, and the fourth, of four or five volumes, to the fluviatile genera.

The Manual of Conchology, completed according to the author's plan, will consist of from twenty-one to twenty-nine octavo volumes, all fully illustrated.

The scope of this great work is described in the "advertisement" or preface of the first number, which was finished and ready for publication in the last week of December, 1878. Mr. Tryon says, the Manual "will include, in systematic order, the diagnoses of all the genera and higher divisions of the mollusca, both recent and fossil, and the descriptions and figures of all the recent species; together with the main features of their anatomy and physiology, their embryology and development, their relations to man and other animals, and their geological and geographical distribution."

The numbers of the first series were issued quarterly. Volume IX was completed December 1887. The nine volumes include 3125 pages of text, illustrated by 680 plates of 12.055 figures.

The first number of the second series—terrestrial mollusca—was distributed January 1885, and thereafter quarterly to the close of Vol. III, December 1887. The three volumes contain 942 pages of text, illustrated by 187 plates of 6,434 figures.

Conscious that he probably might not live to complete his enterprise, but without foreboding, Mr. Tryon interested Mr. H. A. Pilsbry in it. To him he freely imparted his purposes and views in connection with it, so that he might continue the publication, should it become necessary. Mr. Pilsbry, who had the unreserved confidence of the author, has succeeded him in his office and will edit

10

the work according to the plan. It will be published by the Conchological Section of the Academy, of which Mr. Pilsbry is the Conservator.

Mr. Tryon published the first volume of Structural and Systematic Conchology, in 1882 ; the second, in 1883, and the third and last volume, in 1884. The three volumes contain 1195 octavo pages of text, illustrated by 140 plates of 3,087 figures.

During the last ten years of his life, Mr. Tryon wrote 5262 octavo pages on conchology, illustrated by 1007 plates of 21,576 figures. To the labor of composition the business cares of publication were added : he was the publisher of his own works.

Until his admission into the Friends' Central School, October 1850, whatever religious impressions he may have imbibed in childhood, if any, came from the Sunday School and the example and teaching of his parents who were Lutherans. After leaving school, June 1853, he became interested in the Society of Friends and regularly attended its meetings during several years. For reasons, no doubt conclusive and satisfactory to himself, he left the meetings of the Friends, and, from about the year 1876, he was usually present at the stated services of the First Unitarian Church of Philadelphia. When it was proposed, about 1883, to construct a new building for the church Mr. Tryon was chosen one of its trustees. The work interested him. He gave very generously ($1000) in aid of its completion. He was long chairman of the Society's committee on music, and, until his death, was prominent among those who, in various ways, actively promoted the interests of the church.

He was not, however, rigidly sectarian. Knowing that there is difference on every question that interests men, his natural spirit of tolerance swayed his views and conduct relatively to those holding opinions opposite to his own.

He printed for private circulation, a pamphlet entitled, *Church and Stage*, with the motto, *Fiat justitia, ruat cœlum*. It contains twelve octavo pages, and is dated March 15, 1880.

The object of the paper is to uphold the drama as a proper means of popular instruction in spite of its general condemnation by clergymen.

After stating substantially that, in western Europe as well as in ancient Greece, the stage is the off-spring of the ceremonies of public worship—that the mystery play, which followed the liturgical drama, was the first form of the serious national stage in England, France,

Italy, Spain and Germany,[1] he contends that in as much as the theatre has originated independently and exists under many types of civilization—Chinese, Japanese, Indian, Greek, Roman and modern European—and the influence of the Christian Church exerted against it through so many centuries has failed to extirpate it, the institution is likely to continuously thrive. Therefore, instead of persistently denouncing the stage, it would be more politic to kindly endeavor to point out and eliminate from it all acting that is, in any degree, detrimental to morality.

His manner of treating the subject may be seen in the following quotations:

"The first charge is, 'that dramas are frequently immoral stories, abounding in covert or open indecencies of language or action—sometimes actually blasphemous.' We appeal to any regular theatre goer whether his experience does not partially confirm this. Even those who frequent dramatic representations with the intention of encouraging only meritorious and unobjectionable plays, occasionally through ignorance of the matter of some new drama, or misled by uncandid notices of the press, find themselves 'assisting' at representations, quite bad enough to destroy their faith in the theatre. Our own experience, however, and we believe that it will be borne out by the experience of every play-goer who has not depraved instincts, is that plays are usually entirely innocent, and those of a serious character are intended to and do inculcate good morals and right living, that they teach man's whole duty with, (no words are more expressive), dramatic force; that is to say, they make an impression such as can never be made by either reading or lecture; for, to the power of trained declamation is added the verisimilitude of scenery and action. The eye as well as the ear receives and transmits the lesson to the brain and heart. No sermon can be so effectual for good, simply preached from the pulpit as when it is embodied in appropriate action:—that brings it home to us in all its reality; it is no longer a mere abstraction.

The play's the thing
Wherein I'll catch the conscience of the king.

"Such is a good play, better than the best sermon, not only more powerful but more far-reaching in its beneficent mission.

"Then if we take up the clerical charge once more, and agree that the amount of evil done by conveying this indecency or blas-

---

phemy through the vividness of dramatic portrayal is incalcuable; that it familiarizes the auditors with wrong thinking, speaking and doing, and thus lowers the moral tone of the community.' On the other hand, a good play, by parity of reasoning, should have an equally incalculable good influence, and we believe that it has. The vast majority of men [who] are not attracted towards the church, find themselves unable to comprehend its methods, endure its limitations, or perhaps appreciate its motives—and for these, else left without moral instruction, the play yields along with its human interests and entertainment, its realistic teaching by example as well as precept.

"Nay more, the clergyman who objects to the representation of the prayer scene in 'Hamlet,' does not hesitate to read the passage, or to hear it read, perhaps by the very actor who is accustomed to play the part, and who will throw into it all the emotion and all the action that the lecture platform permits him. He will even listen to this recital in the opera house probably, and without alarming his conscience 'because it is not a dramatic performance, but only a recital.'

"Thus, to be consistent, it seems that we must at least tolerate upon the stage, that which we approve in the library or lecture room. But this point is not yet exhausted: there are various conceptions of morality perhaps, and that of the churchman is not necessarily the highest. No one will deny that among theatre-goers are to be found persons who are as cultivated in religion, morals and manners, as tender of conscience, as responsive to the call of duty as any of the abstainers. Is it not rather illiberal then to assume that these persons only visit the theatre because they, in this particular, disregard the voice of conscience? Again, the lower classes of mankind, who frequent the sensational second-class play, who read the equally sensational second-class 'weekly;' are they to be frowned down on account of the vulgarity of their amusements? The uncultured cannot become educated christian people at a bound: generations of refining influences are required to effect the transformation. For these men and women in process of enlightenment, with yet unformed, or badly formed tastes, the theatre is a civilizing agent of far greater power than it is for their betters.

"It may be taken for granted that actors as well as audiences are susceptible to the moral or immoral lessons of the drama, and if, as we assert, the vast majority of plays exert great, though unobtrusive moral influence, then so far as their profession may be supposed to affect their conduct we should expect to find actors respectable and worthy the acquaintance of the pure and noble. But, it will be said, there is abundant evidence that at least many actors are dissolute people, that they live low, vagabond lives, are indecent in language and conduct, drunkards, gamesters, irreligious. The evidence, alas! *is* abundant, and if it could be proven that the proportion of actors who are disreputable is larger than in other professions, we might accept the fact as some evidence of the cause assigned for it; but it is notorious that in all public professions lapses from rectitude are numerous.

" A word in conclusion concerning those who, whilst despising the stage and its associations, yet avail themselves of its fruits. They owe their best music to its inspiration; their best choir singers there received their education; their minister is himself indebted to it, either directly or indirectly, for the force and grace of style and declamation which render him so impressive. Without the stage you would not be possessed of Shakespeare—whose single influence for good has certainly far outweighed all the evil which the theatre has ever done mankind. Those who while discountenancing the theatre, read Shakespeare or hear him read; who listen with delight to the operatic overture or aria; who hang entranced upon the eloquence of the rostrum, are meanly, (I had almost written dishonestly) enjoying the fruits of an institution which they condemn."

Whether Mr. Tryon's championship of the stage be acceptable or not, few persons will fail to perceive in it his philantrophic disposition and love of justice, as well as the degree of his inclination to render homage to the Muses.

To those who would withhold all such matters from a biographical account of a scientest as not pertinent, and to those whose hostility to the theatre is relentless, the above citations may seem too long; but they may be excused. They prove that his mental scope took in very much more than the truths of natural science; that the comparatively inferior and ignorant classes of society had his sympathy, and that he was ready to help improve their mental and moral level. Thus, they indicate a feature of his character not portrayed elsewhere in his writings. None will deny that a feature partly or wholly left out obscures or spoils the likeness, even in a finished painting of a friend.

Mr. Tryon was notably cautious and conservative in scientific work. The personal reputation incident to success he did not appreciate very highly, nor regard to be among the objects of scientific research. Just as a private in the ranks, forgetful of all the labor and perhaps blood he has contributed towards it, delights in the glory of his regiment, wholly unmindful of the personal distinction he may have fairly earned for himself, so Mr. Tryon toiled to promote the welfare and fame of the academy, within the bounds of which he seemed to have merged his scientific aspirations. Few have been like him in this respect; but his example may have followers. Natural modesty, an almost reclusive disposition made him reluctant to hold office. He often refused to permit friends to nominate him for prominent positions in the society, and was apparently indifferent to the honor of membership in other associations. He did not care to publish that he was a corresponding member of the California Academy of Natural Sciences, from December 1862; of the Boston Society of Natural History, from March 1864; of the Royal Society of Tasmania, from June 1886, nor of any other in which his name had been enrolled.

Mr. Tryon's good sense and unselfish nature ; his cheerful, unpretentious deportment at all times, won for him affectionate respect and enduring friendships. Because he was punctual, prompt and efficient in doing, within the limits of official duty, whatever concerned the interests of the Academy, he deserved and had the unreserved confidence of all.

The quantity and quality of work done during his happy career are perennial vouchers of his unremitting industry and varied ability. It is doubted whether a collegiate training and the Master's degree would have facilitated his progress and enabled him to acquit himself better in any sense. A genius for discovering his own deficiencies, and then filling them by opportune self-help, was a practical substitute for an Alma Mater.

Mr. Tryon's abiding desire to increase our knowledge of conchology, which he has done so much to advance, is manifest in his last will and testament, dated March 18th, 1886.

He bequeathed to the Conchological Section of the Academy certain real estate to be a source of a permanent trust fund, the income from which is to be applied to augment the Conservator's salary, to increase the collection of shells, as well as to other purposes, at the discretion of the Section. All profits which may be derived from his conchological works and from his conchological publication business are to be added to the fund.

This provision, in connection with the present vast collections and an almost perfect library, goes far towards establishing in the United States the centre of conchology at the Academy of Natural Sciences of Philadelphia.

Mr. Tryon was methodical in all his ways, and unswervingly firm of purpose. He always did what he believed to be right in face of all opposition; but he tranquilly considered argument against his opinions, and gracefully yielded them whenever he could not answer it. He passed much of his time in the academy at work among its collections and books. For health's sake he appropriated time for daily exercise in the open air, without much regard to the state of the weather. On Saturday, January 28, 1888, while the temperature, ranged between 12° and 17° F. and the wind was blowing freshly from the north-west, he walked briskly in an easterly direction more than a mile, and returning faced the wind. Paroxysms of difficult breathing forced him to stop many seconds, and several times. On reaching home he was much depressed physically; his circulation was abnormally slow and weak, but he soon rallied and seemed to be surely recovering. In the course of two or three days a kind of roseola, to which he had been liable at times since an attack of scarlet fever in childhood, appeared, and towards the last became hemorrhagic. He died February 5, the eighth day after his cold walk

His father, a brother and a sister survive him. His mother died December 23, 1869. He was a bachelor. As far as known he was at no time inclined to change his celibate condition.

Accepting a definition that poetry is merely the blossom and bloom of human knowledge, Mr. Tryon was Laureate of the kingdom of the mollusca. He well knew all its inhabitants—they were thousands—and characterized every typical one in descriptive lines —full of knowledge but without poetic cadence or poetic measure of any kind. But his whole attention was not given to those mollusks. He had eyes for all natural objects. He was fond of flowers, had studied botany successfully, and learned to botanize. In the summer it was his custom to take long walks in the country. On reaching home from those walks he was almost sure to be laden with flowers

and grasses, gathered by the way, some for study in connection with
his herbarium, which was large, and others to bedeck certain rooms
in the house.   And now and then a mineralogist was surprised to
hear him talk so knowingly about minerals.   Indeed, his acquaintance with natural history, generally, was sufficiently intimate to
make the title of naturalist appropriate to him.   His knowledge of
nature and natural things was a pure accomplishment, in no sense
associated with his bread-wining work while he was the successful
man of business.

This imperfect sketch of an eminent benefactor of the academy
is fittingly closed with the following tributary stanzas, written by
his friend, our fellow member, Mr. John Ford, Feb. 15, 1888.


## In memoriam.

As falls the oak, mature and strong in limb,
    A giant 'mong its fellows tall and grand,—
So fell the peer of those whom Science crowns,
    Th' immortal Tryon, type of noblest men.

Not human hearts alone do feel the blow
    That struck him down in life's meridian,—
The leafy woods, the vales, and quiet streams
    Where Nature's gems he sought, alike are grieved.

E'en Neptune mourns the loss of one who knew
    His sea-born children all by sight and name;
And from their games the Tritons sadly turn
    To breathe a requiem through horns of pearl.

His form is gone, but deathless evermore
    On pages manifold his thoughts remain;
And there, like ripened fruits, they wait the hands
    Of all who would their charming flavor prove.

Though well we know the victor's fadeless crown
    His brow adorns, and that he dwells in peace,
Yet do our hearts, remembering the past,
    Still long to meet him face to face again.

## LIST OF PAPERS AND BOOKS WRITTEN
### BY GEORGE W. TRYON JR.

On the mollusca of Harper's Ferry, Va. Proc. Acad. Nat. Sc. Philad. 1861, pp. 396–399.

Synopsis of the recent species of Gastrochænidæ, a family of acephalous mollusca. Proc. Acad. Nat. Sc. Philad. 1861, pp. 465–494.

On the classification and synonymy of the recent species of Pholadidæ. Proc. Acad. Nat. Sc. Philad. 1862, pp. 191–220.

Description of a new genus, (Diplothyra) and species of Pholadidæ, (Dactylina Chilöensis.) Proc. Acad. Nat. Sc. Philad. 1862, pp. 449–450.

Notes on American Fresh Water Shells, with descriptions of two new species (Vivipara Texana, Amnicola depressa.). Proc. Acad. Nat. Sc. Philad. 1862, pp. 451–453.

Monograph of the family Teredidæ. Proc. Acad. Nat. Sc. Philad. 1862, pp. 453–482.

Contributions towards a monography of the order of Pholadacea, with descriptions of new species. Proc. Acad. Nat. Sc. Philad. 1863, pp. 143–146.

Descriptions of two new species of Fresh Water mollusca, from Panama, (Planorbis Fieldii, Amnicola Panamensis,). Proc. Acad. Nat. Sc. Philad. 1863, p. 146.

Description of a new Exotic Melania, (M. Helenæ.). Proc. Acad. Nat. Sc. Philad. 1863, pp. 146–147.

Descriptions of new species of Fresh Water Mollusca, belonging to the families Amnicolidæ, Valvatidæ, and Limnæidæ, inhabiting California. Proc. Acad. Nat. Sc. Philad. 1863, pp. 147–150.

Description of a new species Pleurocera (P. plicatum.). Proc. Acad. Nat. Sc. Philad. 1863, pp. 279–280.

Description of a new species of Teredo, (T. Thomsonii) from New Bedford, Mass. Proc. Acad. Nat. Sc. Philad. 1863, pp. 280–281.

Descriptions of two new species of Mexican Land-Shells, (Helix Rémondi, Cyclotus Cooperi.). Proc. Acad. Nat. Sc. Philad. 1863, p. 281.

Synonymy of the species of Strepomatidæ, a family of Fluviatile Mollusca, inhabiting North America. Proc. Acad. Nat. Sc. Philad. 1863, pp. 306–322.

Synonomy of the species of Strepomatidæ, a family of Fluviatile Mollusca inhabiting North America. Proc. Acad. Nat. Sc. Philad. 1864, pp. 24–48, 92–104; 1865, pp. 19–36.

Description of two new species of Strepomatidæ; Goniobasis Haldemani, Pleurocera Couradi. Amer. Journ. Conchol. I, 1865, p. 38.

Descriptions of new species of Pholadidæ. Amer. Journ. Conchol. I, 1865, pp. 39–40.

Observations of the new genus Io. Amer. Journ. Conchol. I, 1865, pp. 41–44.

Catalogue of mollusca, collected by Prof. D. S. Sheldon, at Davenport, Iowa. Amer. Journ. Conchol. I, 1865, pp. 68–70.

Observations on the family Strepomatidæ. Amer. Journ. Conchol. I, 1865, pp. 97–135.

Catalogue of the species of Physa, inhabiting the United States. Amer. Journ. Conchol. I, 1865, pp. 165–173.

Descriptions of new species of Melania. Amer. Journ. Conchol. I, 1865, pp. 216–218.

Descriptions of new species of Amnicola, Pomatiopsis, Somatogyrus, Gabbia, Hydrobia, and Rissoa. Amer. Journ. Conchol. i, 1865, pp. 219–222.

Descriptions of New Species of North American Limnæidæ. Amer. Journ. Conchol. i, 1865, p. 223–231.

Review of the Goniobases of Oregon and California. Amer. Journ. Conchol. i, 1865, pp. 236–246.

Catalogue of the species of Limnæa inhabiting the United States. Amer. Journ. Conchol. i, 1865, pp. 207–258.

Description of a new species of Mercenaria; (M. fulgurans,) Amer. Journ. Conchol. i, 1865, p. 297.

Monograph of the family Strepomatidæ. Amer. Journ. Conchol. i, 1865, pp. 299–341; ii, 1866, pp. 14–52, 115–133.

An abnormal specimen of Planorbis bicarinatus. Amer. Journ. Conchol. ii, 1866, p. 3.

Descriptions of new fresh-water shells of the United States. Amer. Journ. Conchol. ii, 1866, pp. 4–7.

Descriptions of new exotic fresh-water Mollusca. Amer. Journ. Conchol. ii, 1866, pp. 8–11.

Description of a new species of Rissoa; R. exilis. Amer. Journ. Conchol. ii, 1866, p. 12.

Note on Mr. Pease's species of Polynesian Phaneropneumona. Amer. Journ. Conchol. ii, 1866, p. 82.

Description of a new species of Vivipara; V. Waltonii. Amer. Journ. Conchol. ii, 1866, pp. 108–110.

Descriptions of new Fluviatile Mollusca. Amer. Journ. Conchol. ii, 1866, pp. 111–113.

Observations on an abnormal specimen of Physa gyrina. Amer. Journ. Conchol. ii, 1866, p. 114.

Note on the lingual dentition of the Strepomatidæ. Amer. Journ. Conchol. ii, 1866, pp. 134–135.

Monograph of the terrestrial mollusca of the United States. Amer. Journ. Conchol. II, 1866, pp. 218–277, 306–327; iv, 1869, pp. 5–22.

Description of a new species Columna; C. Leai. Amer. Journ. Conchol. ii, 1866, pp. 297–298.

Descriptions of new species of Melaniidæ and Melanopsidæ. Amer. Jour. Conchol. ii, 1866, pp. 299–301.

Description of a new species of Septifer; S. Trautwineana. Amer. Journ. Conchol. ii, 1866, p. 301.

Description of a new species of Helix; H. Bridgesi. Amer. Journ. Conchol. ii, 1866, p. 303.

On the terrestrial Mollusca of the Guano Island of Navassa. Amer. Journ. Conchol. ii, 1866, pp. 304–305.

Notes on Mollusca collected by Dr. F. V. Hayden in Nebraska. Amer. Journ. Conchol. iv, 1869, pp. 150–151.

Catalogue of the families Saxicavidæ, Myidæ, and Corbulidæ. Amer. Journ. Conchol. iv, 1869, (Append.), pp. 59–68.

Catalogue of the family Tellinidæ. Amer. Journ. Conchol. iv, 1869, (Append.), pp. 72–126.

Descriptions of new species of terrestrial Mollusca from Andaman Islands, Indian Archipelago. Amer. Jour. Conchol. v, 1870, pp. 100–111.

Descriptions of new species of marine bivalve mollusca in the collection of the Academy of Natural Sciences of Philadelphia. Amer. Journ. Conchol. v, 1870, p. 170–172; vi, 1871, pp. 23–24.

Note on Cyclophorus foliaceus, *Reeve* (non Chemnitz) and C. Leai, *Tryon*. Amer. Journ. Conchol. vi, 1871, pp. 25–26.

Notes on Dr. James Lewis' paper "On the shells of the Holston River." Amer. Journ. Conchol. vii, 1872, pp. 86–88.

Catalogue of the family Cyprinidæ. Amer. Journ. Conchol. vii, 1872, p. 252.

Catalogue of the recent species of the family of Glauconomyidæ. Amer. Journ. Conchol. vii, 1872, pp. 253–254.

Catalogue of the recent species of the family Petricolidæ. Amer. Journ. Conchol. vii, 1872, pp. 255–258.

Catalogue of the recent species of the family Cardiidæ. Amer. Journ. Conchol. vii, 1872, pp. 259–275.

Catalogue and synonymy of the recent species of the family Lucinidæ. Proc. Acad. Nat. Sc. Philad., 1872, pp. 82–96.

Catalogue of the family Chamidæ. Proc. Acad. Nat. Sci. Philad. 1872, pp. 116–120.

Catalogue of the family Chametrachæidæ. Proc. Acad. Nat. Sc. Philad., 1872, pp. 120–121.

Descriptions of three new species of marine bivalve mollusca; Crassatella Adelinæ, Lucina distinguenda, Circe bidivaricata. Proc. Acad. Nat. Sc. Philad., 1872, p. 130.

Catalogue and synonymy of the family Galeommidæ. Proc. Acad. Nat. Sc. Philad. 1872, pp. 222–226.

Catalogue and synonymy of the family Leptonidæ. Proc. Acad. Nat. Sc. Philad., 1872, pp. 227–229.

Catalogue and synonymy of the family Laseidæ. Proc. Acad. Nat. Sc. Philad. 1872, pp. 229–234.

Catalogue and synonymy of the family Astartidæ. Proc. Acad. Nat. Sc. Philad. 1872, pp. 245–258.

Catalogue of the family Solemyidæ. Proc. Acad. Nat. Sc. Philad. 1872, p. 258.

On a series of land and fluviatile Mollusca from Utah. Proc. Acad. Nat. Sc. Philad. 1873, pp. 285–286.

The complete writings of Constantine Smaltz Rafinesque on Recent and Fossil Conchology. Edited by William G. Binney, and George W. Tryon Jr., members of the Academy of Natural Sciences of Philadelphia. 8vo, pp. 96+40+8 = 144; plates 3; figures 69. Bailliere Brothers, New York; J. B. Bailliere et Fils, Paris; H. Bailliere, London; C. Bailly Bailliere, Madrid. 1864.

A Monograph of the Terrestrial Mollusca inhabiting the United States. With illustrations of all the species. By George W. Tryon Jr., editor of the American Journal of Conchology; member of the Academy of Natural Sciences of Philadelphia; corresponding member of the Boston Society of Natural History; the Lyceum of New York; the California Academy of Natural Sciences; the Zoölogischen botanischen Gesellschaft in Wien, etc. Published by

the author, 625 Market street, Philadelphia, 1866. 8vo, pp. 159+
XLIV; plates 18, with colored duplicates; figures, 430. Bailliere
Brothers, New York; J. B. Bailliere, et Fils, Paris; Trübner &
Co., London; C. Bailly-Bailliere, Madrid; Asher & Co., Berlin.

A Monograph of the Fresh water univalve mollusca of the
United States, in continuation of Prof. S. S. Haldeman's work, published under the above title. By George W. Tryon Jr. Published
by the Conchological Section of the Academy of Natural Sciences
of Philadelphia, 1870. 8vo, pp. 238, plates 32.

American Marine Conchology: or descriptions of the shells on
the Atlantic coast of the United States, from Maine to Florida.
By George W. Tryon Jr.. member of the Academy of Natural
Sciences of Philadelphia. Published by the author, No. 19 N.
Sixth street, Philadelphia, 1873. 8vo, pp. 208; plates 44; figures
550.

Smithsonian Miscellaneous Collections, (253). Land and Fresh-
Water Shells of North America. Part IV. Strepomatidæ (American Melanians). By George W. Tryon Jr.. Smithsonian Institution, Washington, December, 1873. 8vo, pp. LV+435; 838
figures, intercalated with the text.

Manual of Conchology; Structural and Systematic; with illustrations of the species. By George W. Tryon Jr., Conservator of the
Conchological Section of the Academy of Natural Sciences of Philadelphia. Published by the author. Academy of Natural Sciences,
Corner Race and Nineteenth streets.

Vol. I, 1879. Cephalopoda. 8vo, pp. 316; plates 112; figures
671.

Vol. II, 1880. Muricidæ including Purpurinæ, 8vo, pp. 289;
plates 70; figures 977.

Vol. III, 1881. Tritonidæ, Fusidæ, Buccinidæ. 8vo, pp. 310;
plates 87; figures 1287.

Vol. IV, 1882. Nassidæ, Turbinellidæ, Volutidæ, Mitridæ. 8vo,
pp. 276; plates 58; figures 1345.

Vol. V, 1883. Marginellidæ, Olividæ, Columbellidæ. 8vo, pp.
276; plates 63; figures 1351.

Vol. VI, 1884. Conidæ, Pleurotomidæ. 8vo, pp. 400; plates
65; figures 1550.

Vol. VII, 1885. Terebridæ, Cancellariidæ, Strombidæ, Cypræidæ,
Ovulidæ, Cassididæ, Doliidæ. 8vo, pp. 309; plates 75; figures
1301.

22

Vol. VIII, 1886. Naticidæ, Calyptræidæ, Onustidæ, Turritellidæ, Vermetidæ, Cæcidæ, Eulimidæ, Pyramidellidæ, Turbonillidæ. 8vo, pp. 461; plates 79; figures 1582.

Vol. IX, 1887. Solariidæ, Ianthinidæ, Trichotropidæ, Scalariidæ, Cerithiidæ, Rissoidæ, Littorinidæ. 8vo, pp. 488; plates 71; figures 1991. (The first series will be completed in eleven or twelve volumes).

Second series TERRESTRIAL MOLLUSCA.

Vol. I, 1885. Testacellidæ, Oleacinidæ, Streptaxidæ, Helicoidea, Vitrinidæ, Limacidæ, Arionidæ, etc. 8vo, pp. 364; plates 60; figures 1698.

Vol. II, 1886. Zonitidæ. 8vo, pp. 265; plates 64; figures 2072.

Vol. III, 1887. Helicidæ (begun; to be completed in three or four volumes). 8vo, pp. 313; plate 63; figures 2664.

Third series—Marine Bivalves—4 or 5 volumes.

Fourth series—Fluviatile genera—4 or 5 volumes.

NOTE—The second, third and fourth series will be continued and completed by H. A. Pilsbry, Conservator of the Conchological Section of the Academy of Natural Sciences of Philadelphia.

Church and Stage, Philadelphia, March 15, 1880, (printed for private use). 8vo, pp. 12.

Structural and Systematic Conchology: An introduction to the study of the Mollusca. By George W. Tryon Jr. Conservator of the Conchological Section of the Academy of Natural Sciences of Philadelphia. Published by the author, and issued from the Academy.

Vol. I, 1882.  8vo, pp. 312; plates 22; figures 256.

Vol. II, 1883.  8vo, pp. 430; plates 69; figures 1339.

Vol. III, 1884.  8vo, pp. 453; plates 49; figures 1492.

www.ingramcontent.com/pod-product-compliance
Lightning Source LLC
Chambersburg PA
CBHW032052260626
47157CB00020B/3177